COMBINE IT AND DESIGN IT!

Illustrated by
DYNAMO LIMITED and NATE LOVETT

A GOLDEN BOOK · NEW YORK

© 2018 Spin Master Ltd. All rights reserved.
Published in the United States by Golden Books, an imprint of Random House Children's Books,
a division of Penguin Random House LLC, 1745 Broadway, New York, NY 10019,
and in Canada by Penguin Random House Canada Limited, Toronto.
Golden Books, A Golden Book, and the G colophon
are registered trademarks of Penguin Random House LLC.
Rusty Rivets and all related titles, logos, and characters are trademarks of Spin Master Ltd.
Nickelodeon, Nick Jr., and all related titles and logos are trademarks of Viacom International Inc.
ISBN 978-1-5247-6793-8
rhcbooks.com
MANUFACTURED IN CHINA
10 9 8 7 6 5 4 3 2

Rusty and his robot friends are on the go!

Help Rusty find his best friend, Ruby.

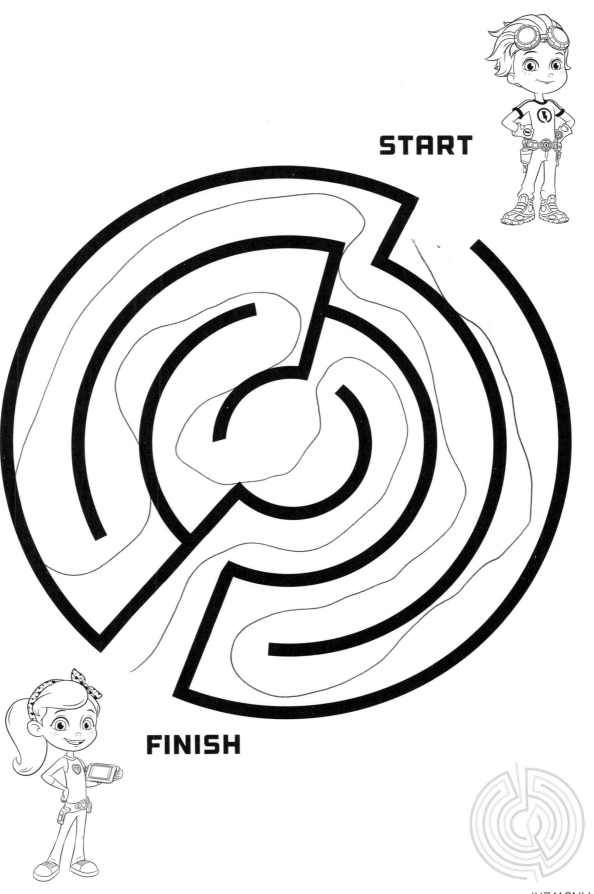

START

FINISH

© Spin Master Ltd.

ANSWER:

Rusty and Ruby make a great tech team!

Botasaur is a giant robot dinosaur.
Rusty and Ruby built him together.

© Spin Master Ltd.

The Bits are Rusty and Ruby's robot helpers.

Flashlight Ray has a single eye that lights the way. Connect the dots to finish this picture of him.

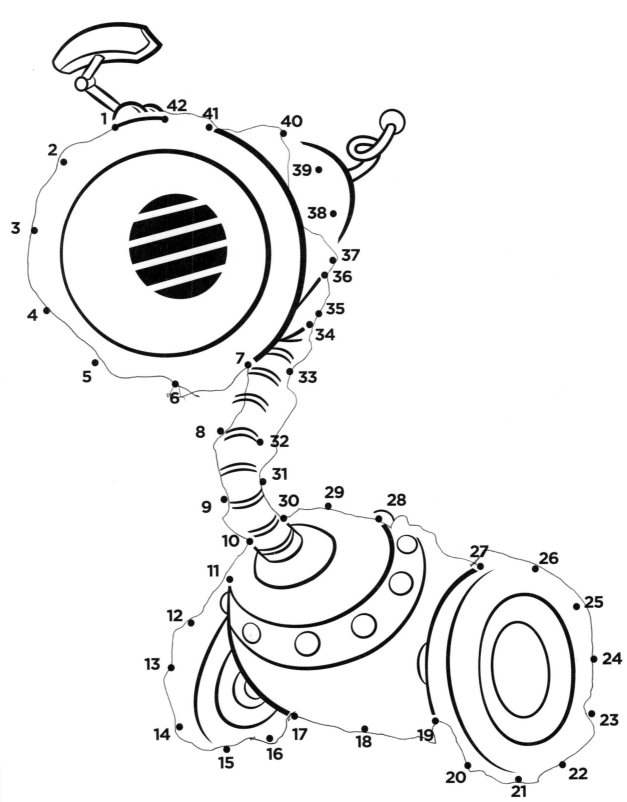

© Spin Master Ltd.

Crush is a vise Bit with
powerful clamping jaws.
Use the key to color him.

KEY
1 = ORANGE
2 = GRAY
3 = YELLOW
4 = BLUE

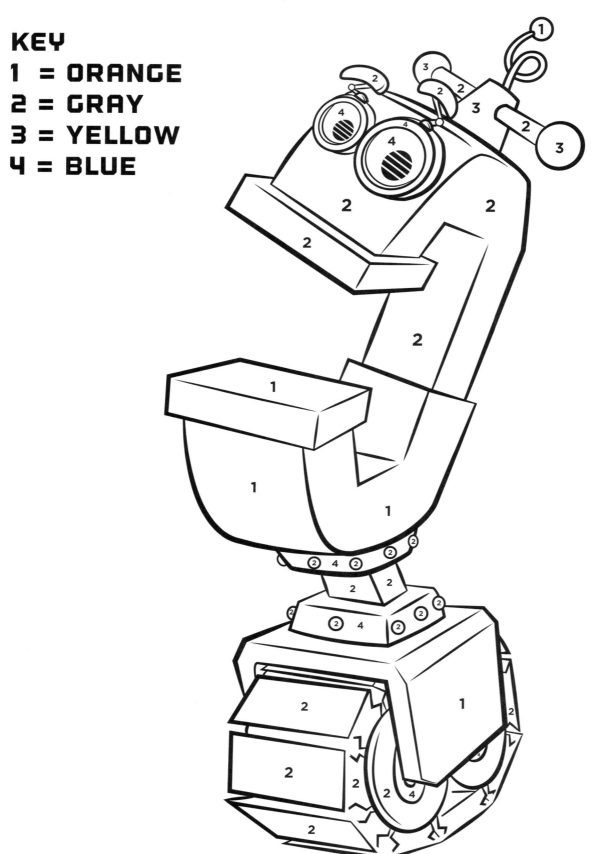

Which path will lead Jack to Whirly?

© Spin Master Ltd.

ANSWER: B.

Match each Bit with its close-up.

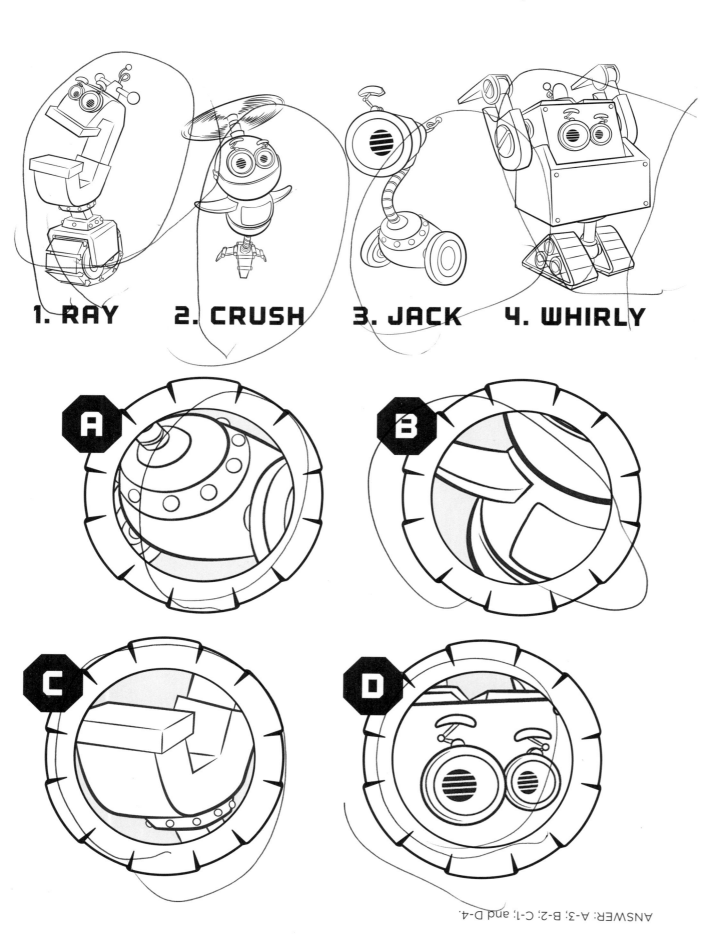

1. RAY **2. CRUSH** **3. JACK** **4. WHIRLY**

A

B

C

D

ANSWER: A-3; B-2; C-1; and D-4.

Bytes is Ruby's playful robotic dog.

© Spin Master Ltd.

Liam is Rusty's next-door neighbor.

Connect the dots to see the tool Rusty uses to project holograms and plan designs.

© Spin Master Ltd.

Which line will lead Rusty to his trusty MultiTool?

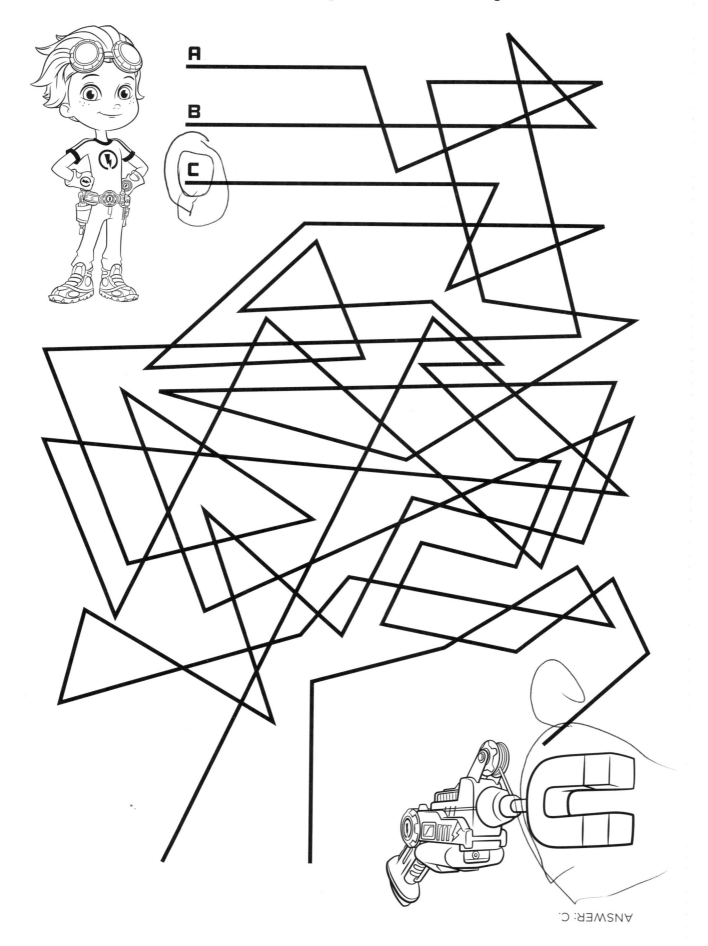

ANSWER: C.

Rusty's jet pack takes him sky-high!

© Spin Master Ltd.

Rusty has a speedy go-kart.

Use the key to color Ruby's buggy.

KEY
1 = RED
2 = BLUE
3 = GRAY
4 = BLACK

© Spin Master Ltd.

Liam loves his trusty trike!

Match each vehicle with its close-up.

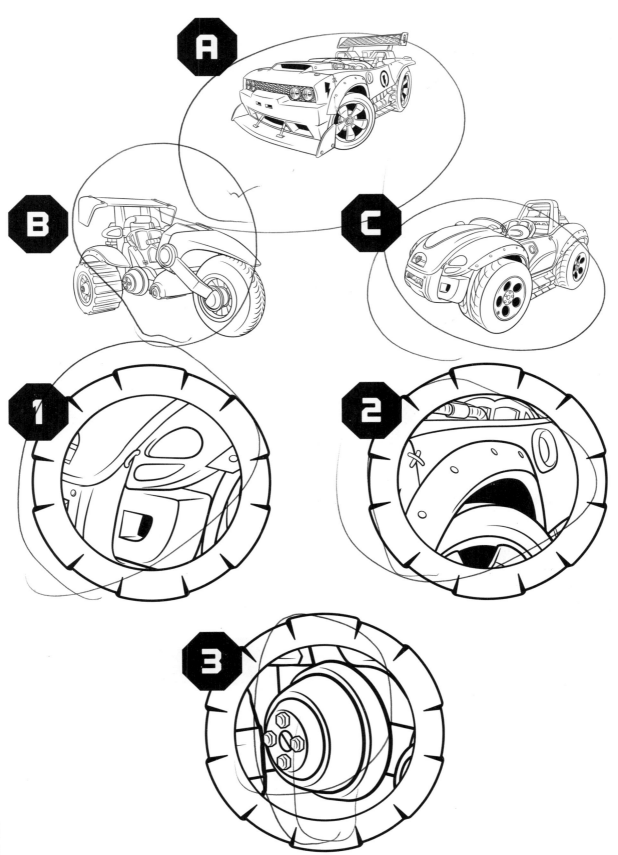

© Spin Master Ltd.

ANSWER: A-2; B-3; and C-1.

Time to bolt!

Rusty and Ruby have a new invention.
The Copycat 500 can make a perfect copy
of anything they put inside it!

© Spin Master Ltd.

Liam wants a copy
of his remote-control car.

Rusty puts Liam's car into
the Copycat 500.
Ruby turns it on.

© Spin Master Ltd.

The Copycat 500 opens.
Three Copy Cars pop out.
They make a huge mess!

After a wild chase,
the Bits catch the Copy Cars.

© Spin Master Ltd.

Rusty puts the Copy Cars in the
Copycat 500, and Ruby presses
the Reverse button. Liam's car is back!

Ruby washes the Bits
with bubbles while Rusty and Liam
clean the Recycling Yard.

© Spin Master Ltd.

Liam thinks the cleanup
will go faster with more Bits.
He puts them in the Copycat 500.

Oh, no! Now there are lots of Bits . . .
and they're on the fritz!

© Spin Master Ltd.

Rusty zooms after the Copy Bits.

The Copy Bits take Mr. Higgins for a crazy ride!

© Spin Master Ltd.

Rusty has an idea. He will catch
the Copy Bits with his magnet crane.

The magnet crane starts to lift the Copy Bits.
Rusty's plan is working!

© Spin Master Ltd.

But then Mr. Higgins drives by,
and the crane cable breaks!

Liam zooms past, playing a song.
The Copy Bits love it and follow him!

© Spin Master Ltd.

Rusty has an idea. He'll catch the Copy Bits
using the magnet crane, the Copycat 500,
some bath scrubbers, and a megaphone.
Combine it and design it!

They make the Super Bit Fix Trap
Action Contraption 5000!

© Spin Master Ltd.

Ruby plays Liam's song over the megaphone.
The Copy Bits can't resist it!

The bath scrubbers
sweep up the Copy Bits . . .

© Spin Master Ltd.

. . . and drop them back into
the Copycat 500! Rusty presses
the Reverse button.

The Bits are back to normal!

© Spin Master Ltd.

The Bits clean up, and soon the Recycling Yard is as good as new!

Rusty and Ruby visit Mr. Higgins
in the park. He is practicing for a
remote-control plane race with
his newest invention, the *Flying Beagle.*

© Spin Master Ltd.

Uh-oh! The remote doesn't work.
Mr. Higgins can't steer his plane!

Rusty asks Whirly to fly up
and grab the *Flying Beagle.*

© Spin Master Ltd.

Whirly uses her grappling hook
to latch on to the plane. But the plane
is too powerful—she can't bring it down!

Ruby looks at the *Flying Beagle* through Whirly's camera. The plane antenna is broken! Without it, the plane can't get instructions from the remote.

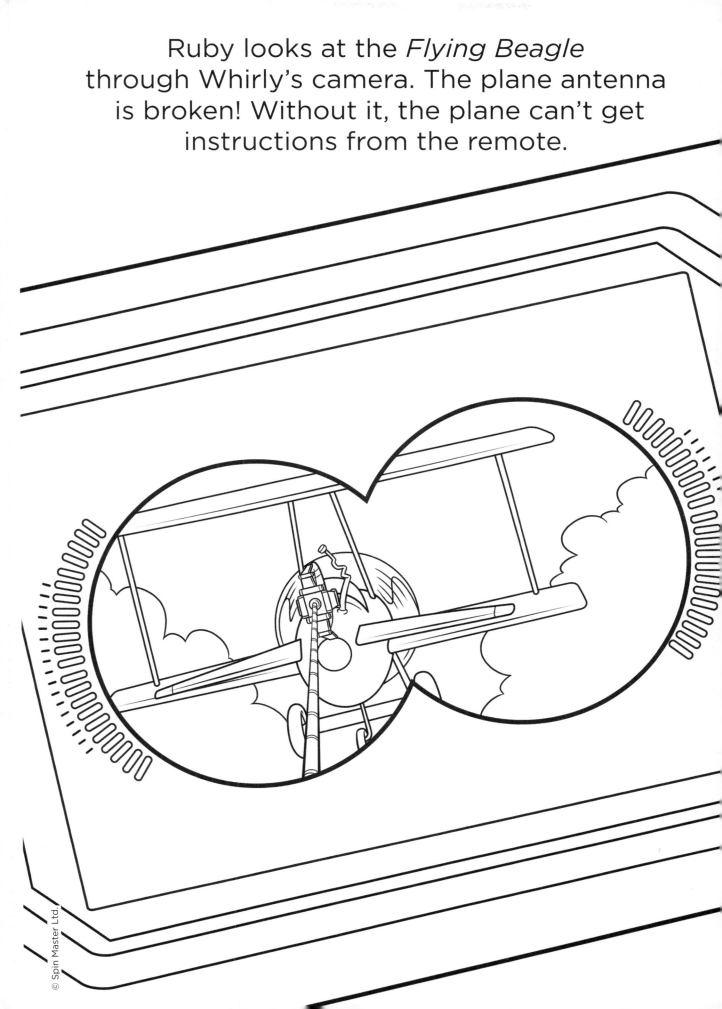

© Spin Master Ltd.

The plane zooms past a teeter-totter.
It's out of control!

Rusty and Ruby will make their own plane
so they can fly up and fix the antenna
in midair. Time to combine it and design it!

© Spin Master Ltd.

First, Rusty needs his turbo trike. Which path will lead him to it?

A ◯
B ◯
C ◯

ANSWER: B.

Next, Ruby needs the teeter-totter. Help Crush and Jack get to it.

START

FINISH

© Spin Master Ltd.

ANSWER:

Connect the dots to see what Rusty uses from the Recycling Yard to complete the new invention.

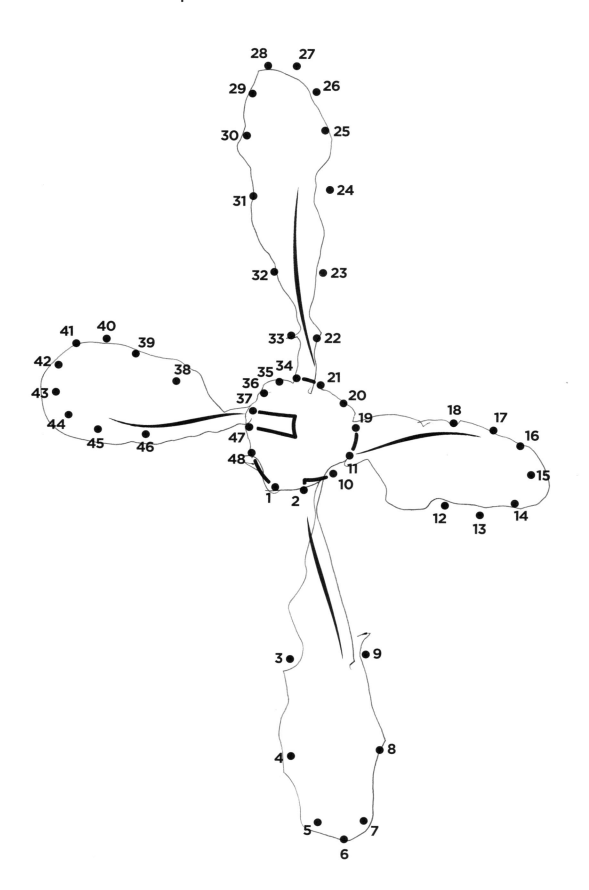

Mr. Higgins has to get the *Flying Beagle* back,
or he won't be able to enter the race!
It's time to head to the Rivet Lab
and get to work.

© Spin Master Ltd.

Rusty modifies the trike.

Crush and Jack bring over the teeter-totter.
Ruby attaches it to the trike
to help balance the plane.

© Spin Master Ltd.

Ruby and Mr. Higgins attach the propeller.

Modified. Customized. Rustified!
It's the Rescue-matic Power Plane 9000!

© Spin Master Ltd.

It's time to try out Rusty
and Ruby's new invention!

Rusty and Crush take off!

© Spin Master Ltd.

Rusty catches up to the *Flying Beagle.*
Crush jumps aboard.

Crush swaps out the broken
antenna for a new one.

© Spin Master Ltd.

Mr. Higgins can control his plane again!

Mr. Higgins enters the remote-control plane race—just in time!

© Spin Master Ltd.

The *Flying Beagle* crosses the finish line first! Hooray for Mr. Higgins . . . and hooray for Rusty and his friends!